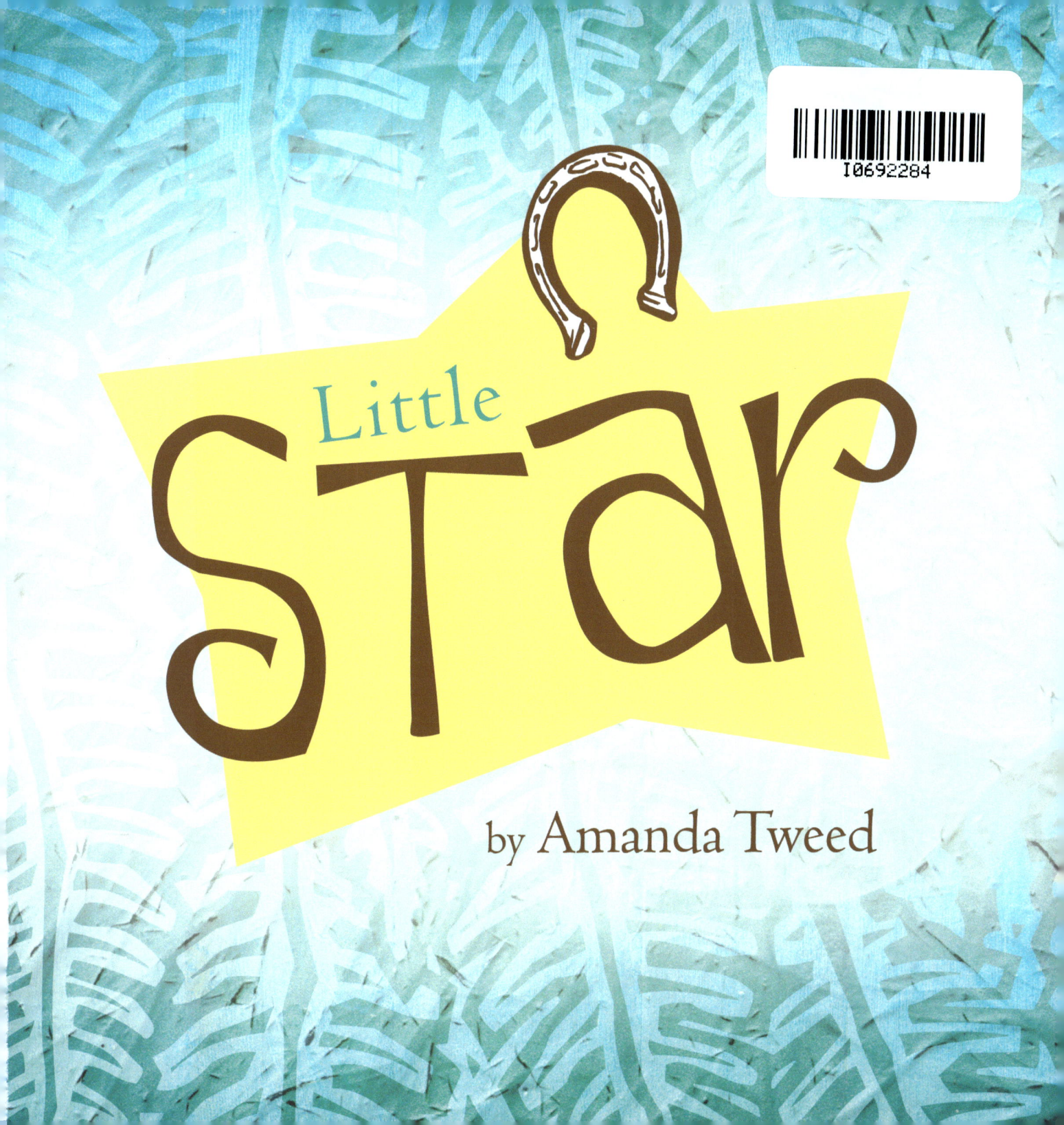

Little Star

by Amanda Tweed

 **Trafford** PUBLISHING®   www.trafford.com

North America & international
toll-free: 1 888 232 4444 (USA & Canada)
phone: 250 383 6864 ◆ fax: 812 355 4082

Early in the morning before the dew disappeared into the sunlight, Mama and Papa Unicorn were taking their morning walk.

All of a sudden they came up on a most peculiar sight. A little unicorn was curled up sleeping in the morning dew.

But this unicorn was different; she was
like no other unicorn they have ever seen.
Instead of a horn she had a white star
where the horn should have been.

"Where are your parents?" asked Mama unicorn.

"I don't know." The little unicorn replied.

"Where is your horn?" Asked papa unicorn.

"I don't think I have one." said the little unicorn.

Mama and Papa unicorn decided that they
could not leave the little unicorn there all by
herself and decided to take her home.

"What about her horn?" Mama unicorn
whispered to Papa unicorn.

"Do not worry it will grow in time." Said Papa Unicorn.

"For now we will call her Little Star." said Mama.

So Mama and Papa Unicorn returned home with
their strange new baby unicorn, just in time
for their little unicorn foals to wake up.

"Who is that?"

"This is Little Star." replied Papa
"She is your new sister."

The little unicorns then gathered around Little Star.

"We are going out to the meadow to play,
would you like to come along?"

"I would love to." replied Little Star."

So they all went off into the meadow.
They had a wonderful time prancing about
the meadow, laughing and playing.

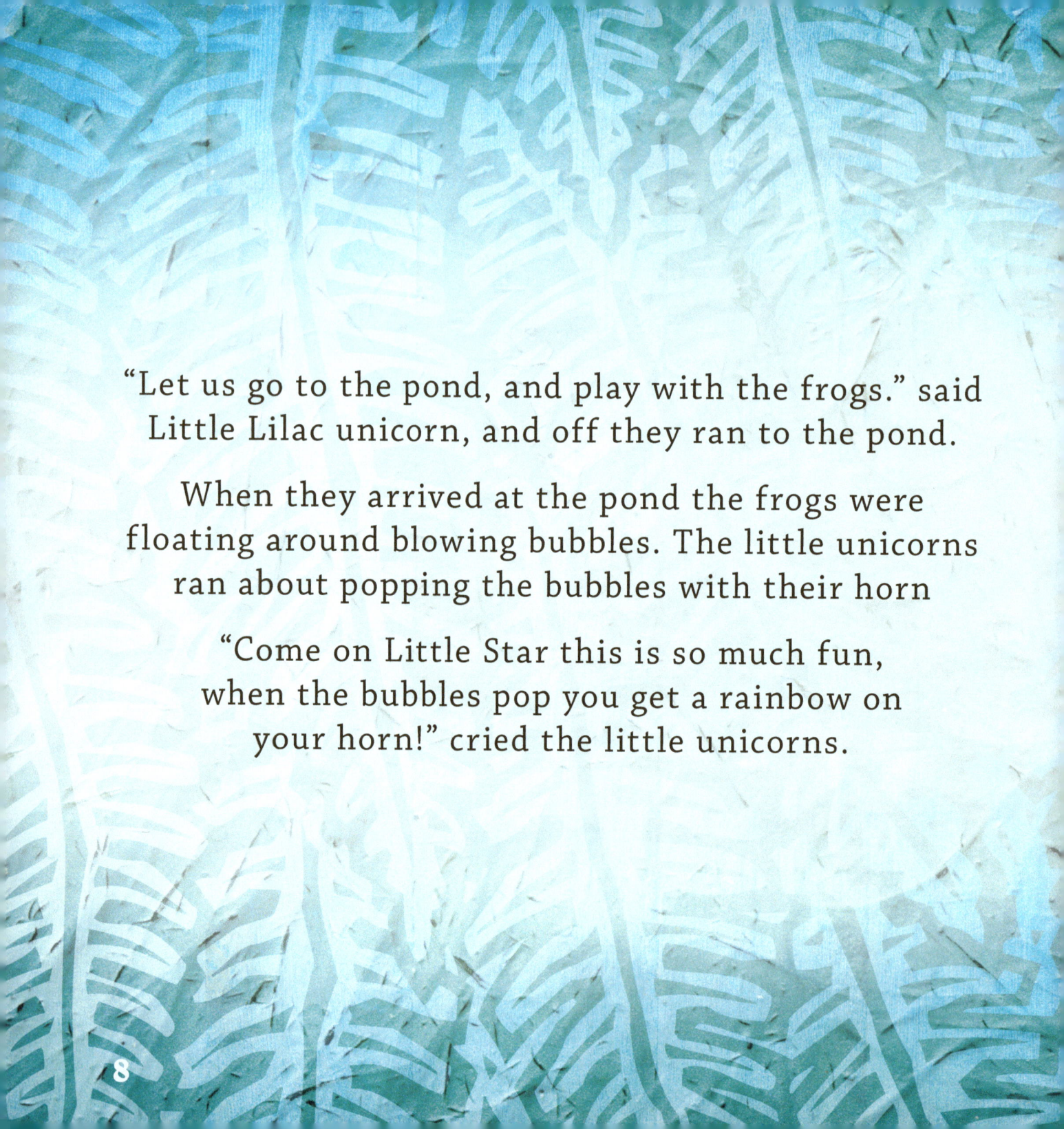

"Let us go to the pond, and play with the frogs." said Little Lilac unicorn, and off they ran to the pond.

When they arrived at the pond the frogs were floating around blowing bubbles. The little unicorns ran about popping the bubbles with their horn

"Come on Little Star this is so much fun, when the bubbles pop you get a rainbow on your horn!" cried the little unicorns.

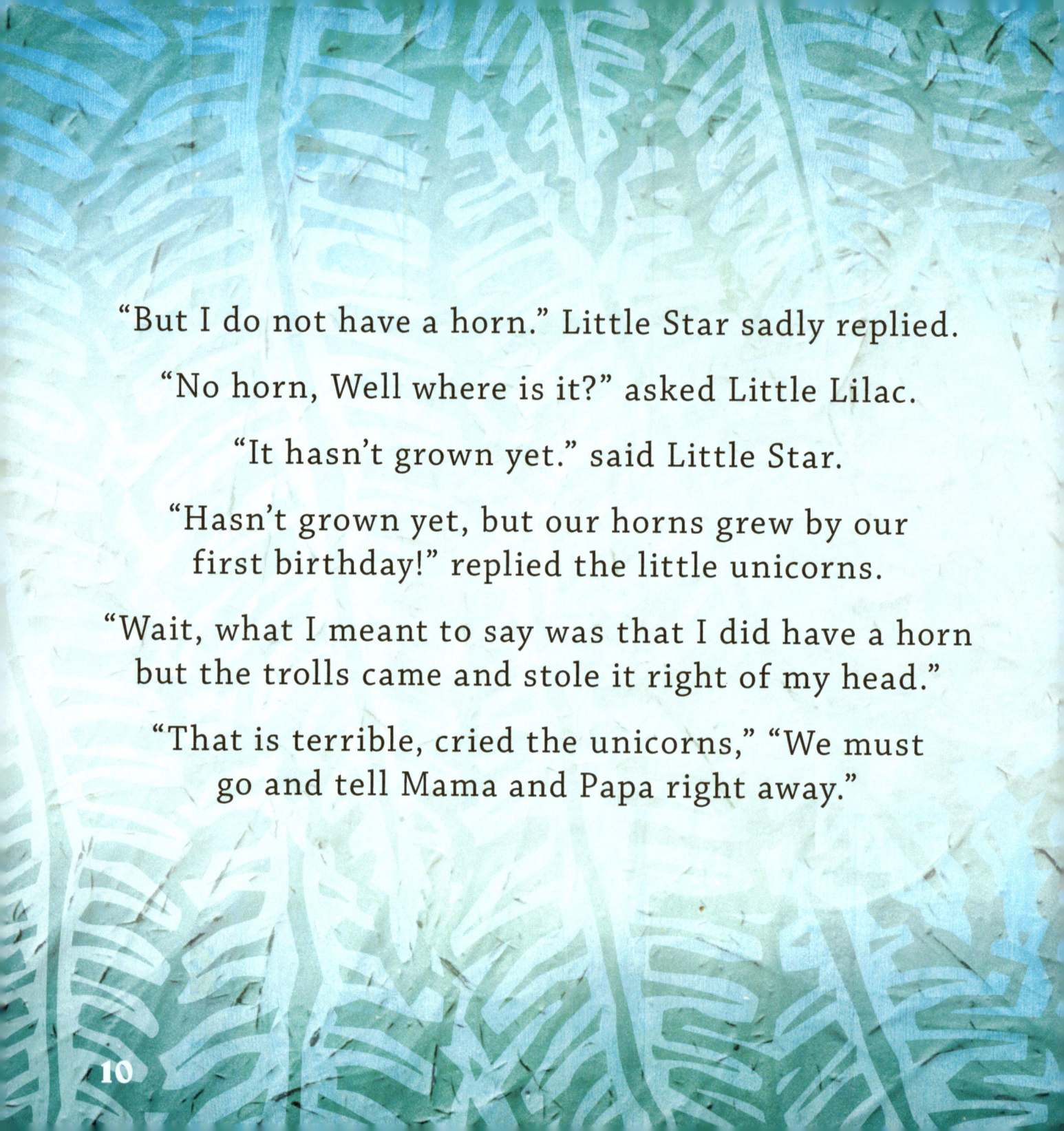

"But I do not have a horn." Little Star sadly replied.

"No horn, Well where is it?" asked Little Lilac.

"It hasn't grown yet." said Little Star.

"Hasn't grown yet, but our horns grew by our first birthday!" replied the little unicorns.

"Wait, what I meant to say was that I did have a horn but the trolls came and stole it right of my head."

"That is terrible, cried the unicorns," "We must go and tell Mama and Papa right away."

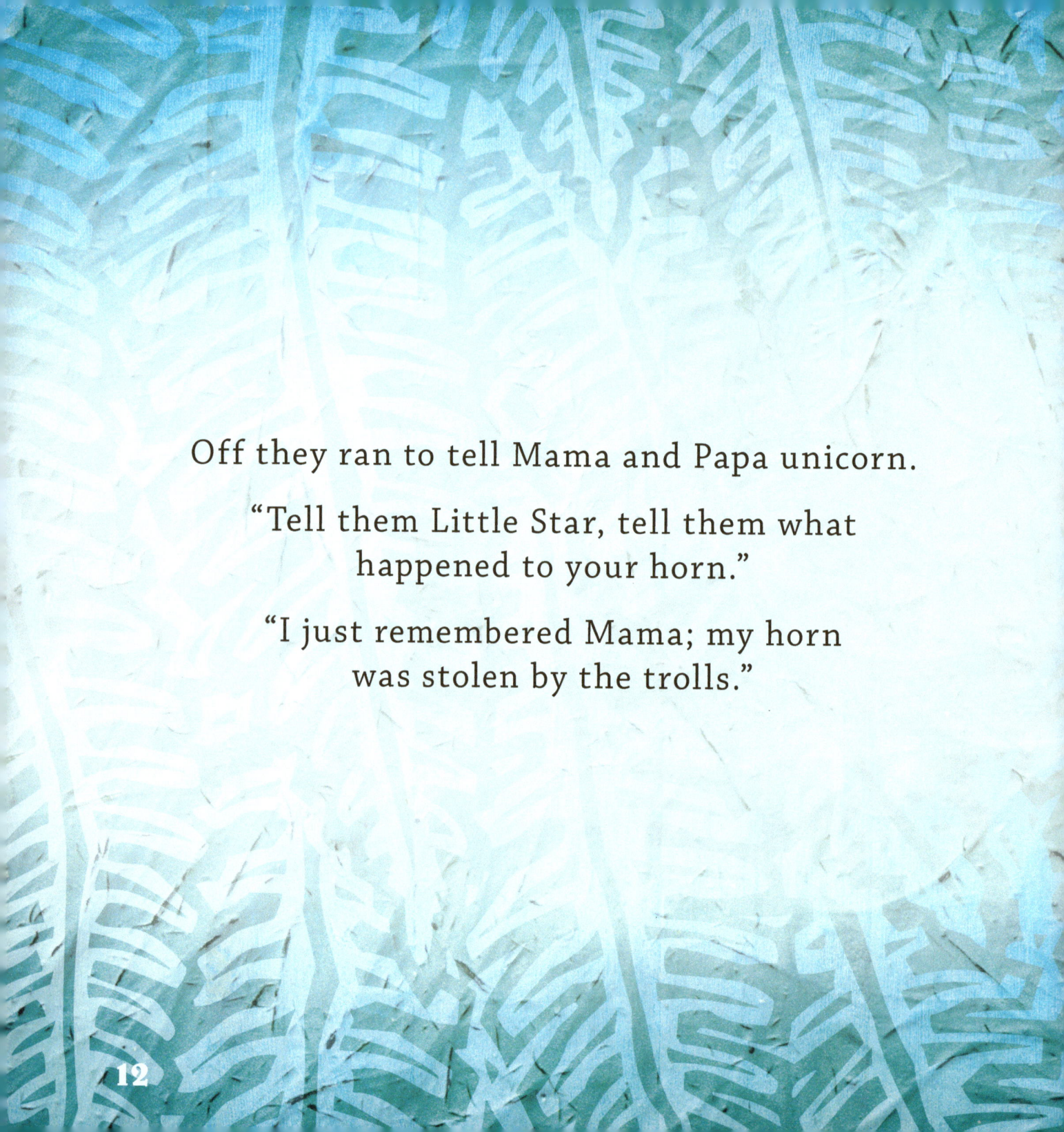

Off they ran to tell Mama and Papa unicorn.

"Tell them Little Star, tell them what
happened to your horn."

"I just remembered Mama; my horn
was stolen by the trolls."

"It is wonderful that you remember little
Star." Said Mama Unicorn, "Let's go to
the troll's house and get it back."

Off they went to confront the trolls.On the way
Little Star realized that she had made a big mistake.

When they arrived at the trolls house
Mama and Papa unicorn demanded that the
trolls, give Little Star her horn back.

"We do not have her horn, replied the trolls
"We have never seen her before."

"Return her horn or we will be forced to
take you to the court of good neighbors,
to be tried by the fairy queen."

"I am telling you we did not take the
horn." Insisted the trolls.

Just then two horses appeared, and they looked just like Little Star. Instead of horns they both had white stars on their head.

"Our Baby!" they cried out.

"Who are you?" Asked the unicorns.

"We are Luna and Marco, we are wild horses.

"We come from the Land of Fey ,one day while grazing in the pasture our little foal ran off chasing some fairies and disappeared."

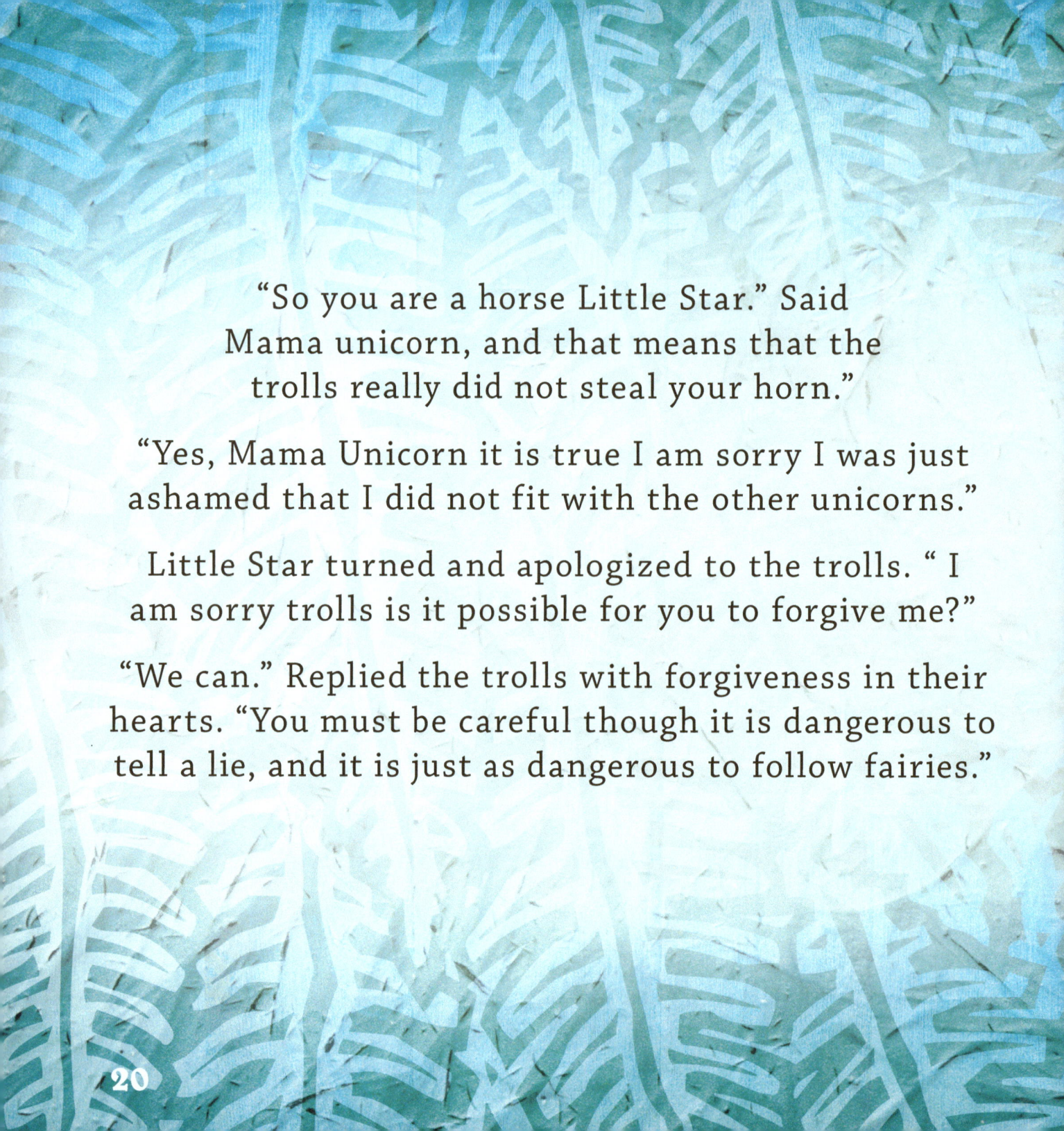

"So you are a horse Little Star." Said Mama unicorn, and that means that the trolls really did not steal your horn."

"Yes, Mama Unicorn it is true I am sorry I was just ashamed that I did not fit with the other unicorns."

Little Star turned and apologized to the trolls. " I am sorry trolls is it possible for you to forgive me?"

"We can." Replied the trolls with forgiveness in their hearts. "You must be careful though it is dangerous to tell a lie, and it is just as dangerous to follow fairies."

The trolls talked with the unicorns and
then went back in their houses. Papa unicorn
drew a picture in the dirt with his horn ,
it was a half circle shape like a hoof .

Papa told the horses that when they go home they
should get a shoe of iron shaped like the picture he
had drawn in the dirt, and put it on their baby horse.

"No magical creatures in the Land of Fey will touch
iron, and your baby will be safe." Said Papa unicorn.

Then the unicorns and the horses said their goodbyes and went their separate ways.

25

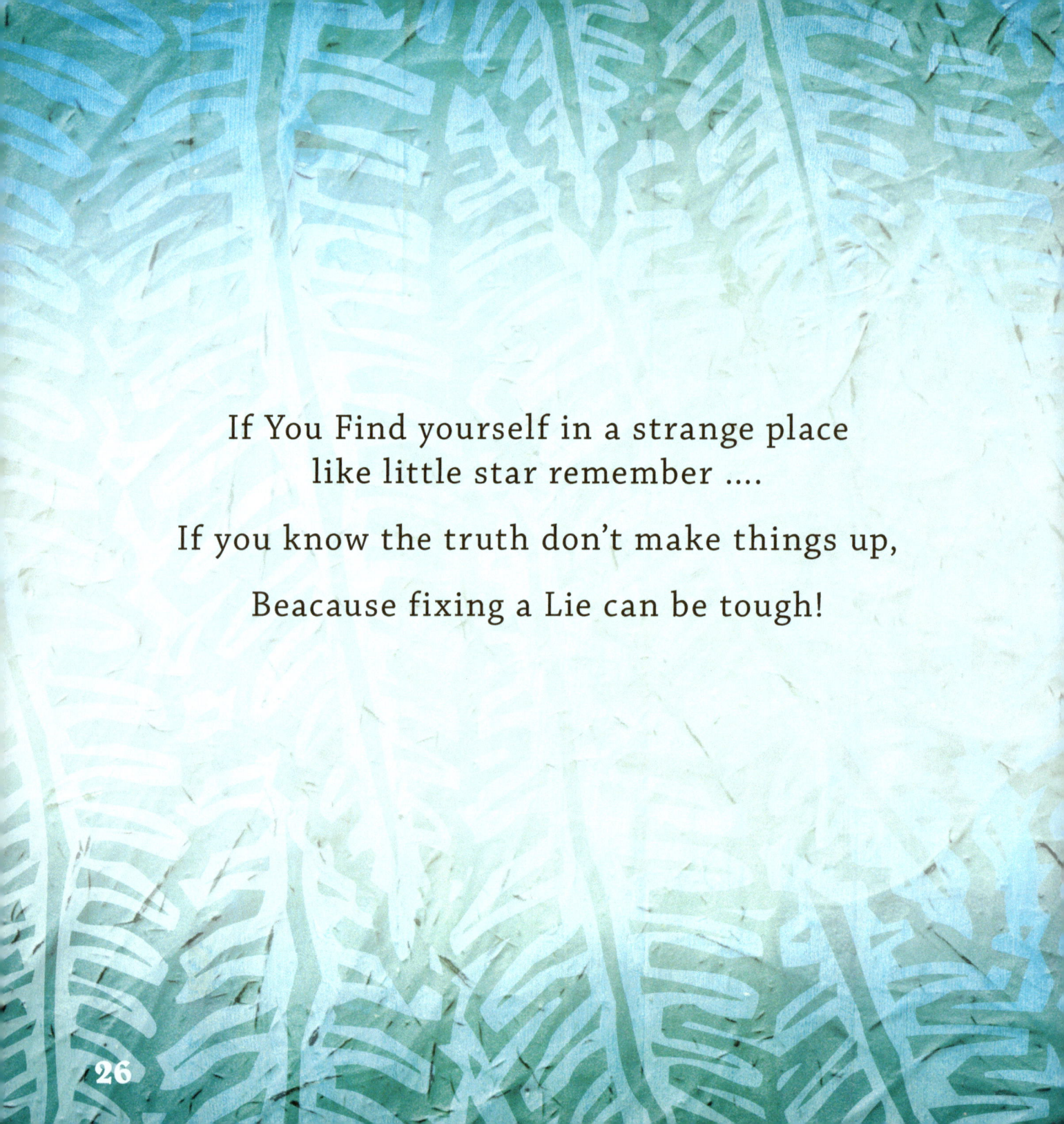

If You Find yourself in a strange place
like little star remember ....

If you know the truth don't make things up,

Beacause fixing a Lie can be tough!

www.ingramcontent.com/pod-product-compliance
Lightning Source LLC
Chambersburg PA
CBHW041721240626
47171CB00002B/19